Color Blind

What A Different World It Would Be

Chenelle Foster

Printed in the United States of America

First printing, 2019

JayMedia Publishing

Laurel, MD 20708

ISBN 978-0-9849290-9-2

Preface

The year 2015 marked the 150th anniversary of the end of the Civil War, a war that changed the course of America history forever. The year 2015 also marked the 150th anniversary of the assassination of President Abraham Lincoln, which unfortunately happened on my birthday, but the point isn't about Lincoln's death, it's about his life. Lincoln fought until his final breath to see that slavery was abolished, and regardless of other things he may have done in his life that people may not approve of, he did a lot to abolish slavery. Just like Lincoln, Harriett Beacher Stowe, Harriet Tubman, Fredrick Douglass, and a bunch of other people worked towards the common goal of seeing all slaves free. There was a lot of work that followed to ensure the right of free African Americans. The Civil rights work of Dr. Martin Luther King Jr., the little Rock nine, Rosa Parks, The Loving Family, and countless others made the world we are in now possible.

Here we are, more than 150 years later and it appears that we have not come as far as we should have. We are still judging people by the color of their skin. A somewhat fascinating thing happened a few years ago, the United States went into World War III over the color of a dress; some people said it was white and gold others thought it was blue and black. Now here's a question no one ever thought to ask: how did it look to the color blind people? Gray maybe? Racism works the same way, everyone looks at someone and sees the color of their skin, but wouldn't this world be much simpler if we were all Color Blind.

CONTENTS

Note To Readers

"Love stories are a dime a dozen, that's why this isn't a love story. It's a life story." This book is completely fictional, but historically based. This is someone's story. I hope everyone who reads this is first and foremost blessed by it, but will also take a step towards looking at people for who they are on the inside and not on the outside. Being color blind isn't about what you think in your head but what you feel in your heart. That is what truly matters. Now don't get me wrong, there is some romance and suspense in this book, but it's not fake. If there is one thing to know about this book, is that it's real and because it's real you will feel something. I decided to not write this book in any particular dialect so all you have to go on are the words they say, not how they are being said. With that, this story does not take place in any particular state or region, but everything is simply referred to as the south and the north. Now I'm gonna stop talking so you can start reading.

In Loving Memory of Michael Issac Thompson.
    (The most color blind of them all)

Acknowledgements

THANK YOU JESUS, I wrote a book. Amen! "I am because He lives."

Mom and Dad you gave me life, the least I could do is use it. You have raised me to be who I am, and I am so thankful and blessed to have you both in my life. Love you!

Chervaun, Gregory, Gerald, Taby, Cap, Stephanie, and Cherie you all are the most amazing family I could ask for. I love you all and hopefully you like my book cause y'all are my number one critiques.

A very special thank you to my Grandmothers Carole Johnson and the late Lucile Foster: the two of you have been so instrumental in my life and in making me the person I am today. I am forever grateful and love you both so much.

Uncle Irvie, thank you for supporting me in everything I do. You are one of my biggest cheerleaders and probably one of the loudest too. I love you so so much!

To all my aunts, uncles, and cousins thank you for the support system you are. I am blessed to have you all in my life, much love. (Special thanks to Uncle Gary and Aunt Alva, Uncle Stanley and Aunt Jill)

To the Thompsons, thank you for all of your love and support. You all have played such a huge role in my life and I can't thank you enough for everything you have done for me. #always7

To my God parents, Uncle Willie, Aunt Belynda, Uncle Wilbur, and Aunt Sonia - You all have blessed me in so many ways and I am incredibly grateful for your support.

Rev and Momma Queen y'all have been a huge inspiration to me and blessed me more than you'll ever know. Thank you for helping me to believe in myself and all I can accomplish. I love you both.

FBCG fam, Pastor and First Lady Jenkins, thank you for the best church fam and creating an environment that allowed youth to grow and learn.

To GOC, BTM, GSS, FRC, and all the activities I have been in. You have shaped a part of me and helped me to reach this point, I am forever grateful.

To my teacher/tutors you all have helped to mold my mind and pour into my life. I am blessed by you and know that this is not only the fruit of my labor but of yours also.

To my friends (you know who you are) you all are the best. You keep me grounded and pick me up when I need it. Thank you for being there for me through everything.

To Worldview Academy thank you for shaping my worldview and teaching me to discern the truth for myself and to most importantly, "pursue wisdom, because she's hot."

Danielle Hooper, you saved my life plain and simple. You're like my second mom/third big sister. I love you so much.

Jeriah, I wrote my book so now it's your turn. Thanks for being my inspiration, love you so much! Now take your bunny nose and be awesome!

To Hannah, thank you for inspiring me to keep writing and not letting me give up on myself. now get writing and finish your book!

Elton, Lol so you are like the best. We had a crazy summer, but I wouldn't trade it for the world. Love you!

Jalen, my main man (aka main guy friend) - Thanks for being one of my top readers. You the bomb!

To the Parkers and Rays, thank you for your continued support. You have no idea how much I appreciate you.

Coach Reece, thank you for being such a huge supporter of me and continuing to push me to keep going and inspiring me to reach my goals.

Coach Philips, thank you for allowing me to achieve one of my dreams and for being so supportive of my writing.

Pastor Cheeks, thank you for your constant care, love, and support. I truly appreciate you being there through my ups and downs.

KM, Lol you'll know this one is yours cause it's the only one whose name isn't spelled out, but thanks for like ya know keeping me alive and all. But in all seriousness, I never would have finished this without you, thank you very very very much!

Lastly, I want to thank any and everyone who has had an impact on my life. I was not able to list every single person but please know I am so grateful for the influence you have had on my life. I love you all so much.

Chapter 1

Beginnings

Home, what is home? To many, home is where their family is, or to others it's where they grew up. To Rebekah Oliver, aka Becky, it's where she was born. Becky was born in the south on July 13, 1940. She was the only child of Ronald and Karen Oliver. The Oliver's saw the world as many people of that time did. They did their best to keep up with society and its changes, but like most white people in the south during that time they were not huge fans of black people.

So when they welcomed their first and only child, a daughter, into the world they came up with a plan. A plan that many years later, would backfire. They made a strong attempt to keep their daughter shielded from the outside world. They didn't want her to know anything about the racial struggles that were taking place in the country. So, the Oliver's did not allow their daughter to play outside with other children, outside of school or to even be a part of afterschool activities. She spent most of her time either at school or alone in her room listening to music on her record player because she wasn't allowed to have a radio. She did that along with reading books that her parents had approved for her. Because of her parents shielding, she was not only completely unaware of the racial differences going on at the time, but lacked many social graces that others became accustomed to through keeping up with current events. That became more prevalent as she got older.

Attending school was not the best experience for Becky. Because of her parent's tight hold on everything she did, Becky was socially awkward and never understood what everyone else was talking about. Then came a pivotal day during middle school when she was given the nickname "Bubble Becky" because she was a little overweight due to her lack of exercise since she was never allowed outside. Over the next few years she became more and more of a social outcast and began staying away from school events unless they were mandatory or the ones her parents would make her attend.

By the time high school came around, Becky was extremely lonely until finally she met someone who would make her world a little brighter. In tenth grade, there was a school pep rally in the gym. The teachers were giving out awards to students based on their performance in the first semester. The student council was given the opportunity to pick a student to give an award to based on a specific list of criteria. And being who they were and Becky being who she was, they decided to give the award to her as a prank.

As she walked up to the podium the crowd began to chuckle, and when she reached out to grab the award everyone pulled out umbrellas, and then the fire alarm went off and then came the sprinklers (this was the original Carrie moment just 20 years before the movie). Becky was instantly drenched from head to toe. She ran off the stage and went straight to her locker to grab her bag so she could leave.

Becky was completely humiliated, as she burst into tears she shortly realized that she was not alone in the hallway, someone was walking towards her. To her surprise it was a girl named Kelly, the student council

Chaplin. Becky started to walk away figuring that she was there to torture her some more.

But that's when she heard, "Are you ok", the last words she thought she was gonna here that day, at least from someone at school.

Becky looked up completely startled, "I'm fine, what do you care anyway?"

Kelly smiled with a seemingly odd smirk, "I just wanted to make sure you were ok, I'm really sorry this happened."

Those words changed the course of both their lives. Kelly's compassion surprised Becky and that was the beginning of a huge change in her life. Kelly asked Becky to join her for lunch the next day, but Becky was worried Kelly's other friends would mock her. So Kelly compromised and decided they would eat together outside.

Becky was incredibly suspicious of Kelly at first because she wasn't sure what her intentions were. She thought they had gone to school together for years, but Kelly had never spoken to her. Kelly rolled her eyes at Becky and informed her that she transferred in at the beginning of the school year. Kelly was from up north and had seen a lot more of the world than Becky. She had taken the position as Chaplin because no one at school would and she assumed it would be a good way to get to know people. Becky was incredibly embarrassed and decided to join her for lunch.

Becky and Kelly parted ways, but their lifelong friendship began and continued from that day forward.

That day and the days after were cemented in Becky's mind for eternity. She and Kelly stayed friends for all of high school. *I won't tell you the whole story now but don't worry you'll find out what all happened later. For now, I will tell you that after befriending Kelly, Becky gained a little more confidence and began to explore different things (again we'll talk about those later).*

In the eleventh grade, the two of them made their mark. They decided that it was time to get revenge on the girls who pranked Becky during sophomore year. Because Kelly was on the student council, she had access to a lot of the rooms around school. So they decided that during lunch time, while the council was meeting, Kelly would excuse herself from the meeting. With Becky's help they would set off the sprinklers in their room while most of the school was outside. After that, the whole council came running outside soaking wet and screaming. The entire school saw them and they became the laughing stock of the school for the next few months.

Unfortunately, one of the girls saw them and reported them to the principal. This was the only time Becky and Kelly ever got in trouble and it did not go over well with Becky's parents (Kelly's parents were pretty chill about it, as they understood the situation). Besides the girl reporting them to the principal told them that they would regret the day they messed with her. Becky and Kelly didn't fully understand how that was gonna come back to bite them but it did *(make sure you remember that it will come up later)*.

By senior year, Becky and Kelly had to start making plans for the future. They didn't know much, but they knew they wanted to get out of their town. So they made a pact to go to the same college. Somewhere up north where they could experience the real world or at least what they thought was the real world. Their parents weren't exactly thrilled about the idea, but they didn't have a choice since the girls had both gotten full rides to school. They were not turning back for anyone, so their parents went along with it, not knowing it would one day tear their family apart.

When graduation came the girls were so excited, the cap and gowns marked the beginning of their new adventure. Before graduation there was prom, they both went and it was an unforgettable experience to say the least. Becky went with Kelly's brother and Kelly went with one of his friends. One of their dates was less than pleasant and unfortunately the night ended tragically, but that story is one that might never be told.

Finally, since they had both received full rides to Racer University, they were ready to go. When graduation came they walked across the stage and went from high school girls to college women. This was their fresh start and after that year they really needed it. With high school in the past and college on the horizon, they were off to face the brave new world together.

Chapter 2

Brave New World

Becky and Kelly arrived in the north in early August for college. They decided to be roommates, since they never actually slept over at each other's houses in high school, because Becky's parents were so strict. Becky, despite being a tenacious person, was at a lost for ideas when it came to college majors. Because she grew up in such a closed environment she didn't know what to expect from others in this situation, but after a while she settled on writing for a major, specifically journalism. She wanted to tell the stories no one else would and push to make the changes the world needed. Becky found the world to be at a crossroads and someone needed to bring light to many situations that were being covered up. She was just the person to do it, or so she thought. So, they began their college lives, while Becky focused on school entirely Kelly was more of the social butterfly. Not too social that her grades suffered though, Kelly was in a pre-law school program specializing in educational and family law.

Despite her intense studies, Kelly always seemed to know what was going on around campus and made sure to find time for those extracurricular activities, especially parties. There were always parties happening on campus and Kelly was at most of them, but every now and then, she was able to drag Becky out of their dorm room and help her participate in what Kelly called the "true college experience". When looking back, they both would agree that their first party was anything but a success.

You see Kelly was considered a "fast" girl in those days, always talking to a new boy every time you saw her. She kept guys on retainer and wrapped around her finger. Becky, however, was the opposite, she would talk to a few girlfriends at a party but never a boy. That was until the one night a very tall, dark, and handsome guy named Eric showed up. There was only one small…or large problem with Eric, and that was that he was talking with

Kelly. The two had met in her economics class at the beginning of the semester and they had really hit it off as friends. Everyone in the school thought they were the dream couple but in reality, they acted more like siblings. Most of their interactions consisted of her poking him, him poking her, and they'd laugh, but that's as far as their romantic chemistry went. The two dated for about a week and then spent the rest of their lives as friends.

That night at the party was the first time Becky saw Eric. Up until that point they had never met in person, only heard each others voice over the phone, because Kelly would just meet him places when they would hang out. So, while Kelly stood in the corner talking with Eric, Becky was trying to ward off the affections of one Sebastian Alexander Portendofer, a nerdy looking, pubescent, narcissistic boy who was desperate to get a date with Becky. During their conversation Sebastian got a little impatient and started making some mildly aggressive motions towards Becky and things almost got out of hand. Fortunately, Eric intervened and convinced Sebastian that maybe Becky was not the girl for him. Thankfully for Becky it worked, but unfortunately for Kelly, this sent Sebastian Portendofer after her.

Following the party, Eric offered to walk Becky back to her dorm and during the whole walk back the two just talked. Becky told him all about her childhood and upbringing, how she spent so much time alone and was so oblivious to what was going on in the world and how that inspired her to become a writer. They talked so much that they didn't realize how much time had passed; as they sat outside the dorms the sun had begun to rise. It was almost six in the morning before they realized what the time was and would have to depart for class in a few hours. That party was the start of their relationship. It was innocent and sweet, but it did not stay that way for long.

Eric and Becky went on plenty of dates after that night. They got to know each other so well they could finish each others sentences. They talked about sports, movies, television, fashion, anything and everything under the sun… well almost everything. They were in what some call the honeymoon stage of a relationship where they wanted to spend every moment of their time together. That is until out of the shadows Sebastian Portendofer emerged to ask Kelly on a date. Kelly tried many means of diversion in order to deter Sebastian's advances, but it was to no avail. He was intense and was not going to take no for an answer. This left Kelly with a choice, go alone with him or convince Becky and Eric to go on a double date with them. So, in reality there was really only one option.

After about an hour of pleading with Becky, Kelly finally convinced her and Eric to double with her and Sebastian. This didn't solve all the problems, in fact it set up for the most awkward date in history.

It was a Saturday right after midterms, Kelly and Becky put on beautiful dresses, and Eric a nice suit. All three sat in suspense waiting for Sebastian to arrive at Eric's dorm so they could go. Then that odd five times fast, two times slow knock came at the door and there was Sebastian in a powder blue tux, completely over dressed, but in no way embarrassed and completely prepared. He escorted them all outside to his car and they left for their evening on the town.

The evening kicked off with a live music event that they all loved followed by a long seven course meal at a beautiful restaurant. And dinner is where everything went wrong… or right. Sebastian tried his best to make meaningful conversation, but when everyone stopped responding he decided to ask questions. He started with simple, "where are you from?" "what's your favorite color?" and so on. As time went by, Kelly realized to her dismay that she and Sebastian had a lot in common and were almost a match made in heaven. Unfortunately for Becky, she realized how little she actually knew about Eric. She knew the basics like his favorite color and stuff, but nothing really personal like where he grew up or anything about his family. Becky tried to stay calm the entire time and not get upset about how little she knew. But that night was a turning point for their relationship.

After the date was all said and done Sebastian offered to walk Kelly back to her dorm room while Eric and Becky stayed at his place to talk. After they left a very heated conversation started between Eric and Becky. Becky wanted to know why he refused to tell her about where he was from or his childhood. After a while, he finally relinquished and told her it was because she would want to know his family and that was not an option. Finally, after a threat to end the relationship by Becky, Eric decided it was time she knew his story.

Chapter 3

A Life To Live

Eric sat her down on the couch in his dorm room. It was time he told her the story of who he was, is and how he came to school.

Eric was from the north. He went to a private school surrounded by white and black people, so race was no big deal for him. But for his family it was a different story. His great grandparents were slaves, and his grandparents were sharecroppers. His parents moved up north a few years before he was born and while his dad worked with white people all the time, they were never invited to their house and they were not allowed to have white friends. Fortunately.... or unfortunately, Eric didn't listen to those rules and that caused a bit of chaos for him and his brother and sisters.

Eric was one of few people who was completely color blind. Red, orange, yellow, green, and blue were complete unknowns to him. For a black individual growing up in the north, racism wasn't as prevalent as it would have been if he was growing up in the south, but that didn't mean it wasn't there. Eric didn't notice the differencebetween races in his mind people were just people. . Not in the literal sense he could tell that black people looked different from white people or Hispanic people just as he could tell that there was difference in colors even if he couldn't see them for what they really are.

In middle school, he wrote a paper about racism and he said, "If only people were all color blind, like I am. When I look at an orange I don't see the bright happiness on the outside, I have to look inside to know what it truly is. The same goes for people: you can't possibly tell who someone is by how they look on the outside, or by what color of skin they have. You must look on the inside of people to know who they really are. And I intend to live my life looking at what's inside people to know who they really are and judging by what's in their heart and not the color of their skin." He saw people for who they really were and who they could be.

Eric had a super sweet heart but also he was a bit unpredictable and he liked shaking things up. In his sophomore year in high school Eric had his first girlfriend and she was……special. His family was anxious to meet her so he brought her home for dinner, and to everyone's surprise she was white. The instant she walked through the door, Eric created a rift in his family that would last forever. His mother and father were furious, his siblings were sent to their rooms to finish dinner. The girl was sent home and he spent the next few hours being lectured by his parents about how wrong it was.

They said things like, "a black man going out with a white woman is like saying it's okay that all those slaves were raped" or that "you are disgracing every black woman and telling them they're not worth anything by going out with a white girl."

In those moments Eric began to resent his parents. How could they judge or even hate someone they didn't know, just by the color of her skin. Eric wasn't an idiot, he knew about slavery and everything that happened and continues to happen, but he wanted to know people for who they are not what their ancestors had done. His dad said white people were born in hate, but Eric seemed to believe hate had to be taught.

So, if at some point white people and black people were taught to hate each other, why couldn't they be taught to love each other.

These philosophies brewed in Eric's mind for years, and when he graduated high school he decided he wanted to study psychology and social science in college so he could understand how people think and help to see each other in a different light. His goal was to open his own counseling practice but to also publish books about racism and reform in order to help bring to light issues in the world to help see the truth.

With that in mind, Eric left for college in pursuit of higher education and understanding. To make a difference in people's lives. And this is how he ended up at school with Becky and Kelly. What he didn't realize is that his platonic relationship with Kelly that introduced him to Becky would change the course of his life forever. Before leaving for school Eric wasn't sure if he ever wanted to go back home. Meeting Becky ensured that he never would, his fate was sealed.

Chapter 4

An Idea or A Solution

The next three years of school passed very quickly. Eric and Becky grew deeper in love. Everyday sharing more and learning more of each other. Since they really knew each other, their relationship grew. Eric found that every time he was with Becky he was more himself. He was more open and accepting of the world around him and who he really wanted to be. It was like all the things from his childhood no longer mattered, all the confusion and misconceptions that were keeping him from accepting every race, every color for who they are was gone. But he knew that being with Becky meant he would have to give up his family, maybe even for the rest of his life.

For Becky things were not so clear cut. She had no way of knowing how her parents would react. Something we didn't know about her and her family is that they had what some would call…… "The Help". Women who would take care of just about everything in their house. Those ladies were the only black people Becky ever saw and her parents didn't necessarily treat them well. Nonetheless Becky had never seen her parents associate with black people in a social setting. The only way to know for sure would be for her to call them and find out. With the possibility of ruining her relationship with her parents, she went to the nearest payphone picked it up and made the hardest call of her life.

Becky's mother answered the phone and they talked about graduation, finding a job post school and all the opportunities that were awaiting her out there in the world. Finally, Becky made a quick transition to the maids that had been working for her family and asking about their wellbeing. Her mother was instantly annoyed, but she answered her questions quickly in an attempt to change the subject.

However, Becky was not finished and in a haste she asked her mother how she would feel if she was dating a black man.

The phone went quiet for a while, then her mother responded, "I know children have been prone to experiment in college and that's fine, but those things will not be tolerated past your education experience. It's time to step into the real world now and there is no place for that in the real world."

Becky couldn't believe the words coming from her mother's mouth. She then went on to ask her mother how would she feel if she were to marry that black man.

In the moment all hope was lost. Becky's mother's words turned from warning to pure disgust and hate. She said, "How completely disgusting of you to ask such a horrendous question! It is absolutely unacceptable for you to think that being seen with a negro man was even a possibility, but for you to present the idea of marrying an animal like that is completely atrocious. Marrying him would be the same as marrying a dog."

Click. The phone went dead. Her mother had hung up. That conversation would be the last she would hear from her mother and family for years.

When Eric heard of the conversation Becky had with her mother he was filled with grief and anguish. Concerned that he was ruining her life, but blinded by love he asked her to marry him after graduation. And so she did.

Graduation rolled around and as the two prepared for the next steps in life something amazing happened a few weeks before. Kelly had gone away for spring break and had returned with this bubbly bright expression covering her face. She and good old Sebastian had eloped and gotten married over break, even crazier than that, she was pregnant. Not really a surprise, Kelly had some positive qualities about her, but abstinence was not one of them. Fortunately, she and Sebastian had been planning to marry long before that and they, like Eric and Becky, were a match made in heaven.

Finally, graduation came, all four walked across the stage receiving their diplomas, but in the audience, were only Kelly and Sebastian's parents. One of Eric's sisters came, but for Becky there was no one.

A few days later Becky and Eric were married and began their new life together. Within a few months they were expecting a child as well. Both couples were overcome with joy about the new experiences ahead of them. Becky and Kelly were excited to be having children six months a part. Eric and Sebastian were excited to be working together. It seemed life was working itself out despite all the hardship they had faced.

Time eventually came for Kelly to give birth and she had an astounding 7lbs. 5ozs. baby boy named Alexander (after his father). He was the pride and joy of his parents, as cute and perky as any baby ever seen. Not long after, Becky had her child. It was a bit of a tense situation as Becky was due six months after Kelly, but her child came five months after.

Becky went into labor on a rainy Friday afternoon. Eric was not yet home from work when she started to experience deep pains and Kelly decided it best to rush her to the hospital. They arrived just an hour before the baby began to push forcefully. Becky was losing a tremendous amount of blood quickly and the baby seemed to have gotten into an unfortunante position.

The doctor was not sure if either would survive, so when Eric arrived he was asked whether they should save his wife or his child. Instantly Eric muttered back, "Both, you save them both, I will not choose." And that is exactly what they did. It took hours but finally the doctor reappeared and told them that they had saved them both.

Eric, Sebastian, and Kelly were overcome with joy so desperately excited to see them both. But there was more news. Because of the complications and procedures that had been performed, Becky would not be able to have any more children. Overcome with so many emotions from horror, to relief, to grief, Eric collapsed. When he finally came to, he was given the task of informing Becky.

Eric slowly peered into her room, he walked over to Becky grabbing her hand and kneeling beside her. He leaned in close to her, touching his forehead to hers and explained what had happened. As Becky's eyes filled with tears he climbed in bed next to her, both with the same thought. The 5lbs. 7ozs. baby girl in the bassinet would be the only child they would ever have. For that reason, they named her Grace, for it was by grace that she was born and by grace that they were able to have the one child they did. Grace would be the love, joy, comfort and peace of their life, there was no doubt about that. But they would hold all the pain and heartache of her life.

Chapter 5

White, Black, Mixed

That baby girl brought Eric and Becky all the joy they needed. The two of them spent the next thirteen years of their lives exactly where they wanted to be, with each other and their little girl. But now with Grace on the verge of her teen years, things would be getting much more complicated. Since Grace's birth a lot had happened. Interracial marriage became legal in all states because of cases like the Lovings, and the Civil rights movement had been a success; things were different or at least they were supposed to be.

Eric had a pretty successful job working as a professor at the University they attended teaching psychology. Becky was spending most of her time raising Grace and helping Kelly with her son and foster kids, but also, she was editor-in-chief of the local newspaper. All in all, their lives were blissful, at least most of the time.

When Grace was younger she was the absolute sweetest girl and she thought everyone in the world was that way. The world she lived in was complete bliss everyone was nice to everyone. She thought everywhere in the world was the same as where she was. Becky and Eric had been raising Grace in a bubble, but not like the one Becky grew up in. Grace knew that there was racism in the world, but she had never experienced the segregation and separation that others did. To Grace it was a thing of the past something that had been overcome. She had no idea how real it was and that the world she lived in was far from what she thought. However it would be a while until she realized it.

Grace had a lot of the qualities of her parents: she was inquisitive for truth and knowledge like her mom, but also rebellious and spontaneous like her dad. The combination of that and Kelly's son Alex created a lot of chaos. Becky and Kelly were inseparable and so were Alex and Grace.

Where they lived, Grace had made a name for herself. She was an ambitious child always seeking to be the best at everything, but never boasting about it. Grace wasn't an attention seeker by any means, she left all that up to Alex. Now he had an eye for flare; he was constantly in trouble with pretty much everyone, there was never a moment that his parents weren't picking him up from a neighbors' for breaking things and even a few times from the police station. The combination of the two of them was pure insanity, the things they did were completely and utterly…well you'll hear more about their adventures later.

The most surprising thought is that at this point Grace and Alex were only 13 years old. Their parents had no idea what to do with them, especially Kelly. By this point Kelly and Sebastian had not only Alex, but four other foster children that they were taking care of. Since both of them were working Kelly was stretched incredibly thin and spent any free time bailing Alex out of trouble. Alex seemed to have a complex about him. He loved all the foster kids his parents would bring home and he took care of them, but every now and then when he wasn't quite getting enough attention, he would get himself into some type of trouble. There were many times where Kelly would get fed up and send Alex to his father's office or over to Becky's to harass someone else. But Becky was okay with it most of the time and would often return the favor by sending Grace over with Alex for dinner. Which under normal circumstances would have been fine, but it seemed the only time when Alex and Grace did not get along was during a meal.

You see Alex had this idea that a man had to take care of a woman when it came time to eat. And well Grace had another idea - that a woman didn't need a man for anything. So whenever they had meals together it always turned into an argument between the two and most often ended when Grace would get fed up and pounce on Alex. On a few occasions she knocked a tooth… or two out. Their tenuous connection would be very important in their future relationship, but no one knew that, so for now it was just the most obnoxious thing to ever happen at a dinner table.

Chapter 6

Home Is Where We Belong

School let out in late May and Becky and Kelly sat in their kitchen trying to figure out something to keep their children busy and out of trouble for the summer. When suddenly the phone rang and Becky sprang to her feet to answer it. The voice she heard over the phone was one she had not heard for years, it was the voice of her mother. Becky's heart instantly sank, the last time her and her mother spoke she was disowned by her family. But the words her mother spoke this time hurt almost as much as the ones she had said before.

Becky's father was gravely ill and they were uncertain if he would make it until the end of the month. Her mother said it was her father's dying wish to see her before he passed, however, her mother was adamant that she did not want to see Becky's husband or child. The two argued over the phone for over an hour. Grace just sat at the table reading, wondering who her mother was talking to. Eric even came home from work to find Becky still on the phone. Not long after he returned, Becky uttered a resounding "We'll see" and hung up the phone. Eric instantly asked her what was wrong, but before she could get the words out she collapsed on the floor in tears and was inconsolable. Eric sent Grace to her room, grabbed a box of tissues, and sat down on the floor next to his wife wrapping his arms around her, trying to understand what had happened. The two sat there for what seemed like days to Grace, but in reality was only an hour. Becky told Eric that she did not wish to speak about it until after dinner when they could be alone. The reasoning for that being that they knew peeking out from her room at the top of the stairs was Grace, wondering what on earth had happened.

So Becky got up, cleaned herself off, and called Grace down to help with dinner. At this point Grace knew they weren't going to tell her anything so she didn't even ask. She merely helped her mom prepare for dinner and ate quickly, stating to her parents that she was eager to return to her book. However, she really wanted them to think she was going to bed so they could discuss the mysterious phone call her mother received. After they all finished and cleaned up, Grace kissed her parents goodnight and raced to her room in hopes that as soon as she was gone they would start talking. Unfortunately for her they knew their daughter and decided to handle the bills first. Grace tried to stay up but fell asleep around 10:45pm, and as soon as they heard sound snoring coming from her room they began to talk.

With a deep sigh, Becky began to explain to Eric about the phone call. Eric sat and listened quietly nodding when needed, when she finished, he leaned in and kissed her forehead and said, "So I guess we are taking a road trip?" At this point we're all on the same page as Eric, but Becky was not, she jumped up and repulsively screamed "NO! How could we?!?!?!" she declared. "After everything they have done, refusing to come to my graduation, missing their grandchild's birth, ignoring us for the past 13 years! I will not give them the satisfaction they want." Becky walked around the room for hours complaining about all the things her parents had ever said or done to her. Somewhere around 2:00 am she took a break and

Eric raised his hand. Becky looked at him puzzled and utterly annoyed. "Why on earth are you raising your hand?!" Eric chuckled, "I wasn't sure if I was allowed to speak so I figured I'd check first." With the most unamused expression Becky walked back over to the couch and sat down next to him. He took her hand and said, "Because they don't deserve it, is exactly why we have to go. Your parents did a horrible thing, but that doesn't mean we have to return the favor." Tears filled Becky's eyes and she rested her head on his chest and said, "Why do you always have to be right."

The next day Eric went into work late. When Grace finally woke up, the two sat her down and explained that they were going down south to see Becky's family. Grace was confused but nonetheless excited for the journey. The rest of the day was spent packing and making arrangements for things while they were gone. Everything was in order until Becky realized she had yet to tell Kelly, a conversation she knew was going to be about as unpleasant as talking to her mother was. With that in mind, she walked over to the phone pulled up a chair, sat down and dialed Kelly's number.

As soon as Kelly picked up the phone she knew it was Becky and started in on a rant about everything that had been going on and how unbearable her husband and son were being. (In reality their relationship was fine, Kelly just had a knack for over exaggerating). Becky sat and listened as always and after Kelly got done explaining to her about this child abuse case she had just finished, she asked Becky how she was doing. Regretfully, Becky told her their plans and Kelly started in on another rant telling her how absolutely horrible of an idea it was and how she would regret it for the rest of her life. It would turn out that she was right about that. Eventually, Becky and Kelly came to an understanding as they always did and hung up the phone.

And with everything squared away the family began their trip down south. They had deemed it their first family vacation. Grace had loaded up the back seat with books, puzzles, and a notebook of questions to ask her parents about their families on the way. Becky tried to answer as many as she could, but eventually told Grace some things should never be repeated and that was the end of all her questions.

I won't bother recounting their entire trip down as the majority of it was uneventful and filled with Grace explaining the agricultural background of every city they drove through and reading excerpts of her book aloud to keep her father awake. However, there is one part of the story that is highly important so I will recount that for you.

As the family began entering into the south they passed by a horrifying sight. There was a black man hanging from a tree looking as though he had been there for days. Grace screamed out in terror of the sight, Eric quickly sped up to get as far away as possible. Once they reached the motel where they would spend the night, Eric carried a still quite scared Grace inside. Becky sat down next to her and Grace latched onto her mother so tightly. The two then began to explain some more about what was going on in the south. Grace asked so many questions, two specifically, "Does that happen up north too?" and "Is someone going to try and do that to you, daddy?" They explained that it does happen in the north but not as much as down south, and then Eric looked her in the eyes and promised that nothing like that would ever happen to him. At least for Grace's sake, he was partially right.

After another day of driving they arrived at Becky's family's home. They pulled up to this beautifully decorated mansion, there were flowers everywhere and lots of people coming in and out of her parents' home. With a deep breath and her husband and daughter's hands, they approached the house and rang the door bell. After hearing a faint, "Coming" the door swung open. Standing in the doorway was a large black woman that stood almost six feet tall, with short curly hair, flour on her face and an apron around her waist. Becky and Eric looked surprised and Grace a little startled. The woman looked them all up and down and exclaimed. "Y'all better come see this, I done won some money!!!"

Chapter 7

Welcome Home

Becky's face lit up and Eric bust out laughing. The woman standing in the doorway was Maggie, the cook/housekeeper that had been around since Becky was a small child. In fact, she was the first person to call her Becky. Becky hadn't seen Maggie since the day she left for school and she had given her some strong advice before she left. She told her that there was so much more to the world than what she knew so she should go find it. Maggie welcomed them inside and explained that the staff had taken bets on whether she would come back to see her dad, and Maggie was the only one confident that Becky would.

Maggie showed them around to see what Becky's parents had done to the house and then she called for Becky's mom. The house fell silent, it was as if they all knew what was to come next. Becky's mother appeared at the top of the staircase. With a somewhat evil stepmother gleam in her eye, she descended each step with her gaze locked on Becky as if she was trying to peer her way into her soul. As she reached the bottom step everyone waited in great anticipation to see what she would say, but before that Becky decided to break the ice.

"Hello mother," were the only words she could get out of her mouth before her mother decided to word vomit on her. "Well, Rebekah it's nice to see you haven't put on too much weight and I see you brought some things with you." Karen wasn't referring to their stuff, she was talking about Eric and Grace. Becky tried to keep her composure and simply replied, "Mother, this is my husband Eric and our daughter Grace." Karen quickly looked them up and down and let out one of the most vicious statements, "Oh! This is the dog who you have been sleeping with? Eric, do you whore my daughter out to your friends or keep her to yourself so y'all can create mix-breeds like this one?"

As soon as those words left her mouth, Grace's eyes began to water and Maggie motioned to one of the other servants to take her into the kitchen. Eric hadn't said a word up until this point, but he couldn't hold his tongue any longer. "Could you be a more evil person? We aren't here to see you. You may not want us here, but Becky's father does and that's who we are here to see."

Karen stared and shouted back, "I don't care! This is my house and no one stays here unless I say so. So get out!"

"Actually Ma'am," Maggie interjected, "Mister Oliver gave specific instructions that they were to stay in the guest house no matter what you say."

With the most disgusted look on her face Karen said, "Fine. Then take the pigs to their pen, I don't want to see them."

With that, Maggie lead them to the guest house and brought Grace out to see them and get settled. She told them that as soon as they are ready, she could take them to see Becky's dad. It took them about an hour to unpack and then Eric decided that they should all rest before going back inside. Grace was very drained from the trip and fell asleep very quickly, so Eric and Becky decided to let her sleep, and go see Becky's dad themselves.

They asked Maggie to come sit in the guest house while Grace slept and so they headed into the house and proceeded up the stairs to the master bedroom. So many thoughts crossed Becky's mind as she walked through the halls of her childhood she could not believe she was back in that house. After a few moments they reached the door to her parents' bedroom, she knocked slowly and after grasping Eric's hand they entered.

Laying in bed was Becky's father Ron, looking quite frail and weak. Becky walked to the bed and sat down next to her father, Eric stood at the foot of his bed. Becky leaned in and kissed her father's forehead, his eyes opened slowly and he smiled. "Ah, my little Rebel, you came home."

"Of course I did I couldn't not come see you daddy." Becky said with the sweetest smile.

"Who is this you brought with you?" Ron said, looking at Eric with a puzzled smile.

Eric took a step closer to the bed and grabbed Becky's hand. "This is my husband Eric, he's…"

Ron interrupted Becky before she could finish, "He's my son." Eric and Becky looked puzzled, they expected just about anything else to come out of his mouth except that. "He's my son, and black, and the father of my first grandbaby I hear. Look, I know your mother had a lot to say about you two getting married, but something about turning my back on my only daughter just never sat right with me. Either way I told myself I wasn't gonna leave this place without telling you how sorry I am. And I wanna spend whatever time I have left getting to know my son-in-law and my grandbaby."

Neither of them could believe what they were hearing. They sat there for hours telling Ron about how they met, how Grace came to be and all about the years they had shared up to this point. The next morning they brought Grace in to meet him. She told her Grandpa all about her life and school and sat and read to him for hours. They ate every meal together for the next few days, the four of them just sitting together, laughing and smiling.

About a week after they arrived, Ron's condition took a turn for the worse and one afternoon he got into a hysterical coughing fit and was never able to regain his breath. Ron passed that evening. Eric, Becky, and

Grace were devastated. After spending all this time away, Becky could not believe that she had so little time with her father. After a few days, Mrs. Oliver began planning her husband's funeral, Becky tried to provide suggestions to her mother on things that would be good to put in the ceremony, but Karen would not hear any of it. The only words she said was that she would allow them to stay as long as they wished since those were her husband's last wishes.

When the day came, the family entered the funeral one by one with the saddest expressions on their faces; all except for Karen that is. For whatever reason she had, Karen refused to show any emotion. Becky and Maggie were complete wrecks and there was a constant stream of tears rolling down their faces. When things finally wrapped up Becky sat at the front of the church. After everyone had left, Grace had gone home with Maggie, Eric walked back inside looking for Becky he knew where he would find her. "Becks, are you ready to go?"

She lifted her head with so much sorrow and regret and said, "Why?"

"Why what?" Eric said as he sat down next her.

Becky took a deep breath and let it out with a big sigh, "why did I wait so long to come back here. He has wanted to make things right with me for years but it took until he was on his death bed for me to come back and finally talk to him."

"I wish I could tell you, sometimes that's just how life goes… we don't get to decide what hand we're dealt we just have to decide how to play it."

Becky looked at Eric with a combined expression of anger, joy, and bitterness. "How can you say that…… is it really that easy for you to detach yourself and give such a heartless comment. Aren't you the first one to always talk about forgiveness and trust and moving forward! You should have made me come back here a long time ago and made me sit down and talk to them! You could have done that, but instead you let me sit at home and grow bitter day after day and then I came here and we talked to him and he let Grace fall in love with him and me forgive him and you let that happen you…you…you…" Becky collapsed to the floor hysterically crying, and Eric did as he always did. He sat down next to her, wrapped his arms around her and pulled her close 'till her head was resting on his chest and sang the words to a song he had heard many years ago.

Welcome Home

"When I learned to love you

it was the easiest thing I could ever do,

cause you let me love you the way I
needed to,

so here in my heart, please stay

here in my life so our love will
never fade,

day by day you and I will never change

as long as we are true."

Chapter 8

Gone Baby Gone

They stayed with Becky's mom for about a week when Eric told Becky that he needed to go back home to continue work. Becky felt strongly that she needed to stay and help her mom settle her father's affairs. That was something they both agreed on, the one thing they couldn't agree on was whether or not Grace should stay with her mother or go home with her dad. The two discussed the idea and decided that it would be safest if Grace went home with her dad. So the next day the two packed up the car and said goodbye to Maggie and Karen. Grace gave her mom the biggest hug and with the biggest goofy smile ran to the car and hopped in. Eric kissed Becky on the forehead and wrapped his arms around her while the two gazed into each other's eyes.

Becky leaned in and said, "Be safe, I love you and I will be home soon."

Eric smiled, "Take your time. Home is always gonna be there and so will I. I love you." The two shared a kiss and Eric walked to the car. Once he got in, he and Grace turned around and waved to Becky as she stood on the front steps smiling and waving back.

Eric and Grace had been driving most of the day and stopped once or twice for food and what not. The two had been listening to the radio and singing all day, and per usual, Grace had a billion questions. She had her dad re-tell the story of how her parents met and then asked the question that just about every dad doesn't want to answer, especially when talking to their thirteen year old daughter. Nonetheless, they were able to agree on one thing that Eric would walk her down the aisle whenever she did get married. Within a few minutes, Grace was out cold as it was going on 11 at night and Eric planned to drive through the night.

Around 2:00 am, their car came up on this group of boys who were walking down the road towards traffic. As soon as Eric saw them he got a bad feeling so he decided to pop a "U" turn and go a different way. As soon as he tried to do that, the boys started yelling and something came flying through the windshield. The crash scared Grace awake and a piece of glass wedged into her shoulder. It appeared as though the boys had been drinking and were throwing bottles at the cars. As soon as the bottle hit and Grace screamed, Eric swerved and ran off the road.

Eric instantly locked the doors and told Grace to get down, but it was no use the boys came running over to the car screaming and jeering.

"Look what we got here boys: a nigger and a mixed mutt!" one of them proclaimed.

"I think this one seems to enjoy humping on things," another one shouted. Two or three of them ripped Eric's door open and dragged him out. Another few went to Grace's side and pulled her out. Eric used all of his strength to fight off the boys and kept screaming to Grace to kick, scream, scratch, bite, and run. The boys continued to make many racist comments about them. Finally, after struggling for a while Eric had made the boys angry enough that they tied up Grace and started beating Eric. They bashed bottles over his head, kicked him, jumped on his limbs, they dragged him through the woods, and left Grace tied up in the car after beating her and burning her skin with lighters.

Eventually she passed out from the pain, but the last thing she saw was her father being dragged away screaming. It took everything in him to stay awake, but Eric was determined to keep fighting to try and save Grace. Eventually Eric found it impossible to stay awake after the boys took him, and he passed out breathing ever so heavily, but still alive.

Morning came and the daily traffic came down the road and saw the car abandoned on the side of the road. One couple pulled over around noon and found Grace passed out in the car, the wife stayed and the husband drove into town to get help. Eventually an ambulance came and took Grace to the hospital, and after a few hours she came to and began telling them what happened. The police were sent to the scene and began searching the woods to find Eric. They also called Becky and had the local police escort her to the hospital to see Grace.

It took a few hours, but finally Becky arrived to see Grace. As soon as she saw her, tears began streaming down her cheeks. She slowly approached her daughter lying in the hospital gurney. There were cuts and bruises on her face, burns everywhere, one of her eyes was swollen for a piece of glass being lodged in it. The doctors were preparing to operate on it later in the day, but for now Becky just climbed into bed next to her and held her.

Grace went into surgery that night and finally woke up the next morning with a patch over her eye. The police came in a few hours later to speak to Becky and she insisted that they talk to her and Grace together. The officer swallowed deeply and stated that they believed they had found her husband. Becky wondered why they weren't sure and he said they needed a relative to ID him. Becky's face instantly changed and Grace looked confused. "ID what?....what are they talking about mom?"

"A body Grace……they are talking about a body." Eric was dead, after he passed out, the boys hung him from a tree. All the life had gone from Becky's face and she just grabbed Grace and the two of them sobbed for hours.

Chapter 9

Stay With Me

It took about a week for Grace to be released from the hospital, because of all the injuries she had sustained during the incident. She was going to be in a wheelchair for a while, and after her eye healed, she would need glasses. She would be considered legally blind in that eye, and she could see shadows and outlines of things, but nothing else. Becky took her back to her parents' because it was closer and an easier trip for Grace. She also didn't know if she could bare going back home to their house without Eric. Becky's mother let them stay not because of Eric or even Becky, but she could not bare to look at Grace in all the pain she was in.

Only a few days after being there, Becky realized she needed to plan a service for Eric. Often she found it hard to muster up the strength to work on it. Maggie helped as much as she could, but spent most of her time taking care of Grace.

Early afternoon one day there was the most obnoxious knock at the door and no one was home so Becky went to answer it. She opened the door a little and the person standing on the other side swung it open. It was Kelly standing there with all her bags and Alex behind her. She came through the door, dropped everything, and immediately hugged Becky, who seemingly embraced her with a somewhat distant expression. Maggie and Grace came back a few minutes later and Alex took Grace out to the backyard as Maggie took their things inside.

Alex wheeled Grace to the backyard by the tall tree in the middle. He grabbed a large blanket and spread it over the grass right by the tree. He then put one arm under her legs and the other he wrapped around her, she put her arms around his neck and with all his strength he hoisted her up and gently placed her on the blanket propped up by the tree.

You could hear the birds chirping and the wind blowing as there were no words exchanged between the two. After thirty minutes or so, Alex reached for his backpack and pulled out a raggedy children's story book and began to read them to Grace. Slowly but surely, she began to perk up and even at some points a faint smile would briefly appear across her face. Eventually Grace dozed off on Alex's shoulder, so he closed the book and leaned his head against hers and the two sat there for the next few hours.

Meanwhile, Kelly and Becky were inside. The two had walked in silence to the sitting room. Kelly just rubbed her hand on Becky's back. You could see the tears forming in her eyes, but she was desperately trying to fight them back. Eventually she turned to Kelly, breathed in deeply and said, "I'm fine."

Kelly's eyes watered and she muttered back to her friend, "No." And with that Becky burst into tears, Kelly wrapped her arms around her as she screamed for Eric.

You could hear her screams all throughout the house. Maggie stood in the kitchen in tears listening to the screams of pain from the little girl she raised. Her mom stood at the top of the stairs with a single tear running down her face. She was so deeply conflicted, everything in her wanted to run downstairs and wrap her arms around her baby, but her prejudice wouldn't allow her. In her mind her daughter had brought this on herself. If she hadn't married a black man, none of this would have happened. So with great pain in her heart she turned from the top of the stairs, walked to her room, and shut the door. The house was filled with the screams of loss for Eric for the next few hours until finally it ceased and the house fell completely silent.

Eventually some semblance of life returned to the house. Maggie began cooking dinner which drew Alex in from the backyard, followed by Grace who had no choice but to go with him. Becky's mother came down eventually, and Kelly emerged from the living room after a while as well, but there was no Becky. By the time they were done eating, Kelly went to go check on Becky, but she had snuck upstairs through the back way as to avoid everyone. Kelly went to Becky's room but she did not respond. She merely slipped a note under the door stating that she wished to be left alone. A few hours later they all prepared for bed. Maggie helped Grace into her nightgown and then to bed, she laid waiting for her mother to come in as usual and say goodnight, but she never came.

Finally Kelly came in and sat on the bed next to her.

"Looks like its just you and me tonight," Kelly whispered.

"It's been just me for a while, mom hasn't come in since…… well yeah……"replied Grace.

With a quirky and unsubtle reply Kelly said, "Well your mom has never been much of a night person, but I'm sure after she gets some rest she'll be back at it."

Grace looked up and said, "You don't have to lie to me Aunt Kelly. I know she's not gonna come tuck me in anymore, and I know why. It's because he's dead. My dad is dead, and anytime my mom looks in my eyes she sees his face. I know she doesn't get out of bed or talk to anyone or do anything anymore. I was there you know, I saw what happened and heard the screams, so don't try and pretend to me like everything is okay, I know its not."

Kelly looked at Grace completely stunned. Grace's eyes watered and Kelly grabbed her, pulled her close, and the two sat like that for hours. Standing in the door was Alex, he watched his mother hold his best friend. Tears began to form in his eyes, but a greater anger began to form in his heart, the fruit of which was soon to be revealed.

Chapter 10

Outcast

It had been six weeks since her dad died and Grace couldn't bring herself to do much of anything, she just laid in bed. Sometimes going downstairs to socialize with Maggie, but never her mother because deep down she knew that it was her fault that her dad was dead.

Kelly spent much of her time trying to keep Becky up and going and out of bed, with things like going grocery shopping or anything remotely close to normal life. Eventually they realized it was about time for school to start so Becky decided to enroll Grace in a local middle school. Meanwhile Kelly spent hours on the phone with Sebastian debating whether or not to enroll Alex in school there as well. Ultimately they decided that it would be best to keep Alex and Grace together. So Grace and Alex would start school together in just one week. Unfortunately Grace didn't know what she was in for, things were a lot different in the south.

The first day of school was nothing new to Grace but this year felt so much different. She knew going into it that every time someone looked at her there was a chance they would know about what happened to her and her dad. Grace was still in her wheelchair so the first day would be more challenging than usual. Alex being the caring boy that he was, pushed Grace around making sure that she got to every class safely.

Things weren't different in the way Grace expected. She never paid much attention to the fact that she didn't look like the blacks or the whites. If someone took a picture of Grace what you would see is a mocha skinned girl with long curly light brown hair. She was the definition of the word mulatto. Her silky skin was just too light for the black people, but just dark enough that the whites would have nothing to do with her either. Grace had never experienced this type of segregation before and it didn't sit well with her or Alex. The two spent most of the day fighting off stares from aggressive older students who resented them purely for how they looked.

By the time they got home, Grace felt even more alone and isolated than before. She came in and rolled straight to her room. Becky and Kelly tried to ask how the day went but they had to ask Alex because Grace wouldn't respond to a single thing they said. Kelly could see this darkness brewing inside Grace, a resentment that reminded her of something that had happened many years before.

Becky let Grace be for most of the day but finally when it was time for dinner she called her, but Grace didn't respond. Becky went upstairs to her room and gently knocked on the door; still silence resounded from the room. Finally out of concern, Becky went in to find Grace facing the window with tears running down her cheeks.

"Grace, babe, what's wrong!?!?" shrieked Becky.

"What's wrong!? What's wrong!? Everything is wrong! You, me, everything" replied Grace as she began to hyperventilate. "Dad is dead, everyone at school hates me because I look like your morning cup of coffee! THIS IS HELL! And its all my fault if dad hadn't been trying to protect me, he would still be alive!"

The cries Grace let out broke Becky's heart to its core. She sank to the floor not knowing how to comfort her daughter. Kelly had been standing in the doorway listening, so she walked over to her friend and picked her up off the ground and walked her to her bedroom. Kelly sat Becky on the bed and told her to let her talk to Grace. "It's time she knew," said Kelly in a solemn tone.

Chapter 11

Help I Need Somebody

Kelly walked into Grace's room and sat down on the bed. "Grace, I know how you feel," stated Kelly.

"How could you possibly know how I feel? Have you ever been responsible for someone's death?" Grace responded with so much spite and anger in her eyes. She didn't expect Kelly's response though. With tears pouring into her eyes, she responded yes, she was responsible for the death of someone she cared about very much.

The story that it was time to tell was that of Kelly and Becky's prom night (that thing we said we'd get back to earlier, well we are getting back to it now). Well the two couldn't get dates to prom so they decided to go with Kelly's brother and a friend of his. The boy had been a long time crush of Kelly's, so when he surprisingly agreed to go to prom with her, she thought it was suspicious but nonetheless she was out of her mind excited. What no one knew is that boy happened to be the older brother of the kids Becky and Kelly had humiliated at school. And he didn't agree to go to prom as a favor, but he did it out of spite. He had his own plan in mind.

The night began with so much joy and bliss, the boys picked the girls up from Becky's house in Kelly's brother's Cadillac. They were decked out in their powder blue tuxedos and the girls had on gorgeous ball gowns. The moms lined up out front for pictures, and eventually they were off for the dance. Kelly's brother sat in the front with Becky while Kelly and her date sat cozied up in the back seat. By the time they arrived at the dance they were fashionably late and strolled in at the perfect time to be the show stopping couples of the night.

About halfway through the night, Kelly's date asked her to go for a walk with him so the two strolled outside. As soon as they were gone, one of the boys they had humiliated went to the coat room and grabbed a pair of car keys. About 15 minutes or so later, Becky noticed Kelly was gone so she told Kelly's brother and the two went to go look for her. Kelly found herself in a rough predicament. She was outside with her date and 3 other boys. You see they had decided the best way to seek revenge on them would be to hurt Kelly. So the boys decided they were going to rape her. Two of them had grabbed Kelly and dragged her into the backseat of the car. She tried desperately to scream but couldn't get any words out, she was overcome with fear.

Becky and Kelly's brother saw some girls inside who previously had dates dancing alone and went to ask them where their dates had gone to. They all replied that they were merely taking care of something that should have been handled long ago. Kelly's brother, being the impatient guy he was, began to yell at them saying things like, "if you know where my sister is, tell me now or you won't live to regret it!" Finally one of them fessed up and said she was getting what a whore like her deserves. In an instant he raced to the coat room, grabbed his keys, told a teacher to call 911, and ran out to the parking lot. Only then did he find his friend on top of his sister in the back seat, her dress hiked up, and she was screaming and crying all at once. He raced over to the car, ripped the door open, threw the guy off her, and began pounding on him. Then the other guys piled onto the fight. It was an all out brawl, but Kelly's brother was holding his own. Eventually the police arrived with an ambulance and as they approached, Kelly's brother stood back and began towards the car where Kelly was. Just as he reached her, his friend pulled out a knife, ran up to him flailing and stabbed him once in the chest and twice in the head. He dropped to his knees right in front of his sister. She saw her brother take his last breath and collapse in her arms.

Kelly and her brother were rushed to the hospital. By the time they reached it, her brother was long gone and Kelly was unconscious. Becky got there not long after with her and Kelly's parents. She stayed at her friend's side until she was released from the hospital. Kelly didn't say much in the days that followed, but she was a changed girl from that day forward.

Grace's eyes were full of tears as Kelly finished recounting the story to her. She couldn't believe what her and her mom had been through. "How" she wondered, how could they be who they are despite having an experience like that. If there was one thing she learned from that moment is that her Aunt Kelly really did understand what she was going through - that and a lot more.

She also realized that there was more to her mother than meets the eye. With that she asked her aunt to roll her down the hallway to her mother's room so she could sit with her. The rest of that day was a quiet one, especially for Alex who had been sitting outside the entire time listening to the story. His eyes lost some of their pure light after listening to what had happened to his mother. That light was replaced with pure hate. He would never be the same again.

Unfortunately Kelly didn't know Alex was listening to her, so when the change began to take place she had no idea where it came from. Her sweet innocent boy changed into a dark brooding teenager overnight. He still took care of Grace but now he had another task on his mind… he wanted to get revenge.

Chapter 12

Sleep Peacefully

As time went on, Grace began to adapt more to the racial separation of the south and she started handling the difficult situation of school much better. Alex, on the other hand, had developed this deep anger because of what had happened to his Uncle. Due to this anger, he decided the best way to handle it would be to take it out on the white families in the surrounding neighborhoods. With that idea in mind Alex gathered materials to set fires across the neighborhood. One here, two there, slowly but surely fires began to surge across the town and singe houses. Nothing had been burned down but many of them were damaged enough from smoke that people could not live there anymore. The police had concluded that the fires were started deliberately, but they couldn't tell by who.

About two months went by and Maggie was out back cleaning out the shed when she discovered Alex's stash of accelerants. If you could have seen the look on her face when Alex came home, you would have been knocked unconscious just by the glare of fire in her eyes. When Alex walked into the house he was met by Maggie. She grabbed him by his ear and dragged him out to the shed, she was screaming belligerently and woke the whole house. Kelly came from upstairs, Grace from the living room and Becky from the study. Maggie threw him down and started lecturing.

"Look at this mess, I can't believe it has been you this whole time! Going around setting fires to peoples' homes. Who do you think you are??? Someone could have been seriously hurt or died!" screeched Maggie. Alex merely looked at her and stammered some unrecognizable words.

Kelly came sprinting clear across the yard and with all her might whacked Alex up against the side of his head. "I can't believe this!" she said. "How could you do this? If the police find out you'll be in jail for years, or worse… life!!! Why on earth would you do this???"

Alex just stared at them all and said absolutely nothing. He sat for a few minutes and collected himself, stood up and walked inside and sat down for dinner. He ate slowly, then stood up, walked into the study, and began writing a letter. When he was done he sat it down on the kitchen table and walked out the front door. Kelly, Becky, Grace, and Maggie all watched completely stunned. Kelly rushed over to the counter to read what the note said.

It read, "I'm sorry for starting the fires, I never meant to hurt anyone, or maybe I did. All I know is that it was the one out of control thing that I was able to control in a way. Since moving here, I feel like everything is all wrong. I understand that I have to be here, but after hearing what happened to my mom and uncle I just have this hate deep down inside me and I don't think its going away. This seemed like a constructive thing to do with all that hate, but honestly I'm not sure. Anyway I'm sorry and if you all want to turn me in it's fine."

Kelly crumbled up the letter and sat down on the steps. Much of what ran through her mind was memories of how she felt that sad day her brother died and a piece of her was stolen. But most of it was how terrible her son must feel knowing that happened to someone he loved. It would be nice to say that was all of Alex's bad boy antics, but that would be far from the truth. It was only the beginning of a dark road that eventually others would join him on.

A few months or so later Becky found a job working at the local newspaper as the editor. She wasn't necessarily telling the stories she wanted to, but she was getting to write and that brought a lot of joy and happiness to her life. And after the year she had she really needed it. She worked half days and mostly nights so she could be around to help Grace when she got home from school.

Meanwhile, Kelly had gotten a job at a local firm and was slowly rising in ranks and becoming one of the best lawyers in town. By the time Christmas came around, Sebastian had joined them and moved his practice and started establishing a new clientele. Christmas was very quiet and things were much simpler than years before, but it was exactly what everyone needed, especially Grace. Kelly had a picture taken of Eric, Becky, and Grace and had it made into a large portrait painting to go over the mantle of the house. Then she had a small photo of Eric and Becky made for Grace to put on the nightstand next to her bed.

Everything was finally looking up for once, then New Year's Eve came. Becky had been working late the nights leading up to New Year's Eve, against the recommendations of her friends and family, especially because of the editorials she had been writing on the racial struggles surrounding their community. But that night she had some work she just had to finish. Around 7:00 pm this odd smoky smell took over the paper backroom. Becky realized she was not alone in the shop. There were about 5 or 6 large men in the room.

"Look at this one, she likes being humped by dogs. Guess she won't mind if we take turns on her," one of them said laughing. Two of them came across the room, grabbed her, and threw her to the ground. They had started a fire in the back room and were burning the equipment. They tied her to the desk and gagged her.

"You should have known better," one yelled, "If you play with animals, we will treat you like one."

Tears rolled down Becky's face and you could see her fight slowly drifting away. Suddenly, two of the guys began pouring oil all over her, kicking and smacking her. It was a grotesque display of inhumanity. Just as one began to unbuckle his pants, one of the other men ran into the room saying the fire was spreading and they needed to leave. And so they did. They left Becky tied up, screaming as the fire slowly spread and overtook her body.

Grace, Kelly, and Alex were home and heard the sirens of the fire trucks heading down the street. Alex peered out the window and made an incidental comment that it looked as though they were heading to the street where the newspaper was. In an instant, Grace rolled herself outside and began rolling down the street as fast as she could. Kelly followed with Alex and Maggie. Eventually Alex grabbed the chair and began pushing and running. They got to the shop just as the firemen had finished extinguishing the flames. They then realized that there was something in the room. In that moment every emotion one could possibly feel hit at once. Grace realized what she saw, it was the charred corpse of her mother tied to the table with her mouth stuck open as though she had been screaming.

Kelly instantly sank to the ground and Maggie rushed to her side, while Alex grabbed Grace's hand and she sat in shock unable to think or even process what was before her eyes.

That day was permanently etched in her mind forever and cemented the worst year ever in Grace's mind. In just 5 months her mother and father were both gone. Everything she ever knew had been ripped from her in an instant. The world was crashing down and she was slowly being suffocated.

It was about 2 or so weeks 'till the closed casket funeral for Becky. Kelly got up and spoke on Grace's behalf and on behalf of Becky's parents. Grace hadn't spoken a word since, all she did was write. Everyday without fail she would sit and write one letter, fold it up and put it on her mother's bed. She continued this trend for months and slowly Kelly became more and more concerned about her silence. It was as if without her parents, Grace was cutting herself off from the world and choosing to live in the delusions of her mind where they still existed and everything was fine.

Finally the school year was over and Grace was sitting in the living room, Maggie brought her some food for lunch when Becky's mother walked in. "Grace, this silence has to stop, it's not what your mother would want!"

Grace looked up and you could see rage fill her face, "How would you have any idea what my mother would want! You threw her away like she was disposable trash and wanted nothing to do with her! You know nothing about the last 15 years of her life, you have no idea what she would want!!!" Grace screamed at the top of her lungs. The room stood still and everyone was amazed. Kelly approached Grace and attempted to say something, but no words came just tears, as she leaned in to hug her.

They say time heals all wounds, and that was going to have to be the case for Grace who decided now to be called Gracie because that's what her parents called her each night before bed. As days passed, Gracie became more vocal and more defiant. At first Kelly let everything go, assuming it was because of her hardships, but things were getting progressively worse. Especially since Gracie had been doing physical therapy and slowly regaining the mobility of her legs. Not only were her words cutting like daggers, but she was beginning to be able to use her fists to strike fear into others around her, especially at school. It could be said she was turning into a grade A bully with one goal in mind: to cause as much pain to others as she had been feeling.

Chapter 13

Listen To Me

In the six months following the death of her mother, Gracie did daily physical therapy to regain her use of her legs. It was as though with every step she took towards walking was a step towards becoming a more aggressive and bitter child. Between Alex and Gracie, Kelly and Sebastian had their work cut out for them. They were in a constant battle with both of their teens. One day it would be a meeting with Alex's parole officer (that's right, Alex got 16-month probation for starting fires) or the principal at Gracie's school; the two were constantly getting into trouble.

Kelly decided that it was probably time for some tough love to get the two of them out of their self pitying phase. Although the truth was Gracie had every reason to hate the world, it took her parents from her and almost completely destroyed her life. But what she couldn't understand was why she was acting out the way she was. It would have made sense if she was taking it out on the jerks at school, but she was torturing the people who were just like her. Its as if she knew that the people who hurt her were untouchable so she took on the motto of "if you can't beat them, join them."

Sebastian took on a different tactic for dealing with Alex. The two went for a walk through the park and Sebastian sat Alex down on a bench and took out a pocket knife and handed it to him. Alex looked terribly confused and just stared at his dad. Sebastian took off his glasses and said probably one of the most profound things he had ever said in his life (considering most of the things he said were disconnected fragments about some medical diagnosis or slightly narcissistic statements about his intelligence).

"Alex, my dad gave me this when I was 13. He told me whenever I walked my sisters anywhere it was my responsibility to take care of them and keep them safe. I felt this terrible weight on my shoulders my entire life to protect them, my mother, and everyone. Well, one day when I was about 17 and I had to take my college entrance exams, my sisters walked themselves home and they got attacked by some boys who hated Jews. They pushed them down and my youngest sister got this huge scar on her leg. I felt entirely guilty for weeks, until my dad sat me down and told me this: 'You aren't responsible if you're not there.'

And the same thing goes for you. You weren't there when what happened to your mom happened, so there is nothing you could have done about it. I know it makes you angry. It makes me angry to think about it too, but we can't change the past. What we can do is be there for her on the bad days and remind her how loved she is."

Tears slowly filled Alex's eyes as he looked up at his dad and wrapped his arms around him. Sebastian continued with this, "Now for the tough love part, you need to get your crap together and stop causing all this trouble. There are no excuses for what you have been doing other than plain foolishness. Using what happened to your mother as a reason to do this is absolutely despicable and I can't believe you would ever do such a horrible thing."

Sebastian had never spoken this way before…to Alex or anyone for that matter and it caught him completely off guard so much that it was like being hit over the head with a brick. But it worked. Alex took what his father said to heart and realized he was being incredibly selfish and just down right horrible. His behavior didn't resolve immediately but slowly overtime things began to get better and he started actually taking responsibility for his actions and how he treated people.

If only Kelly's conversation with Gracie had gone so well. It was by no means that simple, because unlike Alex, Gracie had every reason to be as bitter and hateful as she was. Kelly thought she had only one option left: remind Grace that despite how bad someone has it there is always someone who has had it worse. Life is the greatest gift someone could ever have and it should not be wasted.

Gracie came home from school one day aggressive and throwing things around the house. Maggie was in a frenzy about her behavior and her and Kelly had spent the morning talking about how someone needed to talk to her. So when she came stomping through the house Maggie decided it was time. Kelly stood up to go talk to Gracie, but before she could Maggie stood up and yelled across the room, "Little honey bring yourself here right now." Maggie had never yelled at Gracie before so she figured she shouldn't test her luck and Grace came over. "The two of us are going outside to talk. Don't nobody come bother us" exclaimed Maggie. And so they went hand in hand outside to "talk."

Maggie walked Grace outside with this dark look in her eyes as though she was about to take her out of this world into the next. Grace looked more scared than ever before in her life, as Maggie let out a deep sigh and said some very intense words.

"Listen to me, little girl. I know you have had one heck of a year, but trust me there are people who have had it far worse than you. Don't you think there are people out in the world that have suffered more than you? I know it's been painful but this self pity you have been walking around in is not okay. I don't know if you're aware but people have been through worse than you. Hell, between the 150 years of slavery in this country and the decades of torture the Jews went through. If everyone walked around like they have a right to treat people wrong because of what they have been through, the world would be a much different place. So there has got to be something going on more than any of us can see, so I suggest you get this off your chest or so help me I will do it for you."

Gracie looked up at Maggie with a dark angry gazed stare in her eye. You could see she was on the brink of tears just as she lifted her head to respond and uttered the most heinous response.

"Go to hell…"

Maggie looked utterly stunned. Gracie walked away as though she had seen a ghost. Internally every thought coursing threw her mind was surrounding her parents' deaths, as they did everyday. She thought about the words Maggie had said and wondered what the real reason was behind her behavior. She thought maybe it was her way of coping with the trauma or possibly something deeper. Either way, she knew she was by no means done with her behavior.

Chapter 14

Lost And Found

It had been a few weeks since Gracie's conversation with Maggie and she hadn't shown any signs of improvement in her behavior. She was suspended from school twice in the past few weeks. The principal was convinced she was in need of some deeper help than what the school could give her and if there were anymore incidents then she was going to be expelled.

Kelly had no idea what to do at this point. Talking to Gracie was pointless, it was as if she was in her own world and completely unconcerned with anything. Anyone that saw Gracie could tell that there was something eating away at her, but she refused to acknowledge anything. Maggie told Kelly what she told Gracie, but obviously it was to no avail.

Everyone assumed that things could not possibly get any worse, until one day Gracie didn't come home. Kelly and Sebastian sat up for hours waiting for her, but she never showed. It was as if she vanished into thin air. Kelly's mind immediately jumped to the worse and she assumed she had been kidnapped or something. After no word from Gracie by the next morning, they went to file a missing persons report with the police. Unfortunately, no one was interested in looking for the mulatto kid from the family who had caused all that trouble.

A few days passed and with no word from Grace, Kelly gathered a few friends and began searching for her. Day and night for almost a week they searched neighboring towns, canvassed stores, and prowled through the woods seeing if there was any sign of her. Finally after ten days Kelly had given up hope. She sat with Maggie in the kitchen her eyes bloodshot from crying so much, all she could think of is how she had failed her dearest and closest friend. Then suddenly the most unexpected thing happened, the front door swung open and in walked Gracie…

At this point since she had been missing for so long, it probably would have been better if she came in covered in dirt or with some elaborated story about being kidnapped, but that wasn't the case. Gracie walked in without a scratch and calm as ever. She came in, looked at Kelly and Maggie and said not a word, simply nodded and walked up the stairs to her room.

Kelly charged after her with the rage of God in her eyes. "You better have a damn good reason as to why you were missing for ten days!" Kelly screamed.

Gracie looked back at her and mumbled. "I had some thinking to do."

"Thinking!?" Kelly yelled back, "Thinking about what!?!"

"My parents." Gracie said with a shrewd smile and tears slowly filling her eyes. "I'm sorry… I'm sorry for everything… for the terrible person I've become and all the horrific things I've done. I just… I just can't… for the life of me get rid of this burning hate in my heart."

"Hate for who... or what?" Kelly responded.

"My parents. I hate them." Gracie stated as she sank down to sit on the bottom step. "They knew the world we lived in would never accept them. They knew that horrible things would come from them being together, yet they chose to do it anyway. Why?!!? I don't understand and I have been trying to figure it out but I can't. It's all wrong they should have never been together, and I should have never been born!" Tears began pouring down Gracie's face. You could see the pain she was feeling in her entire body. Kelly grabbed her and held her in her lap rocking back and forth trying to calm her.

Kelly responded with a soft tone, taking a deep breath before speaking. "Oh my sweet, sweet girl. Yes, they knew everything that could come from them being together, the good and the bad. But they decided that the good far outweighed the bad. You see, despite all the hurt and harm that came upon them, the greatest accomplishment they will ever have is you. They created life, and more importantly a life that will live on and share their legacy so others can know what happened to them and how two people's love changed so much. You see that's what it was, love that brought and kept them together. More than the love everyone talks about, it was patience, kindness, selflessness, forgiveness, life and so much more. Your parents had one of the best qualities known to man - the ability to see past race and into the heart."

Those words resonated with Gracie from that day forward. She was constantly reminded of the color blind love her parents had for each other. Her behavior began to improve and soon she was no longer a troubled student at school. She actually began to enjoy it and learning became a crucial part of her mental recovery.

Gracie would never fully be able to move on from losing her parents the way that she did, but she did learn to turn the situation into a positive and help her parents legacy to live on.

Chapter 15

Free At Last

It had been fifteen years since Gracie, her mom, and dad had moved to the south and her parents died. In that time, she graduated high school and graduated top of her class at college. Her later years of life were not as hectic as the earlier ones, but nonetheless she was still learning and growing and understanding what being color blind truly meant. Nonetheless, when she was asked to come back and speak at graduation that is exactly what she talked about and it went something like this:

"In 1865 Abraham Lincoln died for the abolishment of slavery. In 1968 Martin Luther King Jr. died for Civil rights. In 1965 my parents died for the right for people to see them as God does. Equals. Dr. King said he wished for the day his children could be judged by content of their character and not the color of their skin. I wish for the day when people realize what love is, that love is not only patient and kind but unconditional, love doesn't know skin color or complexion it knows no boundaries and never fails. I look at the world today and people say black lives matter and they do. They say white lives matter and they do. They say blue lives matter and they do. I say all lives matter because they do. The war on slavery was won in 1865, the civil rights movement ended in the 70's. The fight has been won, it is time we start acting like it. If you don't act like a victim no matter what anyone does to you, you can't be one. When I was younger I used to think my mulatto skin was all that mattered. But as I grew up, learned, lived, and loved, I became color blind and realized it does not matter what the outside of you looks like. But it matters what the inside of you lives like. Life is hard, there is pain, but if you don't look beyond color you will never live."

This speech became the school's most well remembered graduation speech of all time. Gracie's words resonated with so many people that day, but most of all they touched

Kelly. She knew Becky and Eric would be so proud of their little girl and all she had become.

Gracie and Alex finally began dating in college and were married after graduation. Kelly and Sebastian went on to adopt three more children along with Gracie and started a non profit in honor of her friend. Through the years they continued to be there for Gracie and Alex and helped them to develop a love and passion for helping those of mixed race become more accepted into society. They also took Maggie in with them and cared for her 'till the day she died. And after 50 years of marriage, Kelly died of cervical cancer and Sebastian passed of a broken heart not long after.

Gracie and Alex went on to be married for 63 years and had 8 children and 37 grand kids. The two went around telling the story of their love, and their parents' love. It was after the day she lost her father that Grace realized the worst day of her life, gave her the greatest gift. Her sight may have decreased, but from that day on, she understood what it really meant to be color blind.

Behind The Story

Growing up I've known a few people that came from mixed families and in those families, I always saw this beautiful undying love. There was one family that I got to know their daughter very well. I got the idea to write this book before I knew her, but the inspiration for some of this story definitely came from her family. This family is a true example of being color blind. This couple met in a mattress store and from there an epic romance sparked. They navigated through many ups and downs, but their commitment to each other, their children, and God shown so brightly and was an example of true love through the highs and lows of life. Color Blind doesn't even begin to describe them.

About The Author

Chenelle Foster is a Maryland native. She is the daughter of Gregory and Carole Foster and has 3 older siblings and 2 nieces. She graduated from high school in 2017 after being homeschooled her whole life and is currently pursuing a Bachelors of Arts in Theatre with a minor in Information Systems. Her goal is to one day own her own multimedia arts center and work with Foster children.

CPSIA information can be obtained
at www.ICGtesting.com
Printed in the USA
FFHW021930261119
56125217-62264FF

9 780984 929092